'PEACHY GIZZARD AND THE SPHERES OF GLAMMETH'

BY

Andrew Coulthard

Brought to you from:

ANDREW COULTHARD

Peachy Gizzard And The Spheres Of Glammeth

1. Meetings

Peachy Gizzard - I first saw him in the shadow of a mal-placed faux renaissance statue at the National Vegetable Museum in Hexham, Northumberland. I've always been fond of that museum, not so much for its extensive collection of legumes, but rather for the restful quality of the architecture. All those Thompsonesque flourishes; the indoor waterfalls, the eerie dead-end annexes shaped like eviscerated body parts and those magnificent vaulted spaces intended for significant, impromptu meetings between strangers. So very wonderful!

I didn't know him then, nor had I ever heard of him. As a stranger he was not particularly prepossessing; an older man with worn, drab clothes and a battered briefcase, grey of eye, stooped of shoulder, grizzled of thinning hair and lined of florid face. He hadn't noticed me at that point and seemed rather preoccupied. I soon lost interest in him and was reading the labels on a glass case of rare Venezuelan pigmy zucchinis when somebody cleared their throat at my shoulder. Looking up I found myself gazing into Peachy's rheumy eyes.

"I was young when it all began," he announced in a voice both mellow and yet gravelly, as if the soul to whom it belonged were of the genteel kind, while the body in which it was housed possessed rasp-like edges and suffered from a surfeit of phlegm.

"Yeah?" I responded, not really knowing what else to say.

"Yeah," he echoed. "Had no idea about anything, but you don't when you're young, do you? All that soon changed though."

He grinned then, a feral light creeping into those bloodshot eyes. The effect transformed his deeply lined face. Flaking, near scaly lips drew back to reveal large, brown teeth, which had been filed into points at some distant temporal juncture for reasons I could only guess at. It was at this moment that I began to find his proximity and aspect truly unnerving. Yet despite my discomfort part of me still believed it sensed something good, kind and gentle within that disturbing shell.

"Don't fret, my dear," he rattled in an effort to reassure me. "I'm going to tell you a little story." And with that he seized my arm and wrested me off toward a row of wrought iron divans at the far side of the hall. I was alarmed, but found myself unable to resist him as if an unseen power were at work, sapping my will and forcing my body into compliance.

"The name's Peacham, Peacham Gizzard," he rumbled, flopping down onto a divan.

"Mine's Gloria," I offered in a quiet voice.

"Pleased to meet you, gal. Call me Peachy; most do."

"Alright," I agreed sitting down beside him.

"Let's have a look at you!" he said grabbing my arm again, his eyes roving over my face. "Hmm, yes, Gloria would be about right. Young, just as I was when my tale begins; that's good. Eyes like dark gold, golden brown complexion and all those blonde curls, I bet when the light hits you it transforms you into a pillar of..."

"*Mr Gizzard*...Peachy, you're making me feel very uncomfortable," I complained pulling free of his grip.

"Yes of course; sorry. I get a bit carried away sometimes. Well to business and that business is a matter of stories or one story in particular to be frank. My story is, of course, only one of many, but of all the folk on this old earth I chose you to tell it to and do you know why?"

I shook my head, already falling back under his spell.

"Pity. I don't either; I was rather hoping you could help me out there." He seemed crestfallen, but quickly regained his spirits. "Well, never mind. Now listen carefully: Appearances can be deceptive. In my youth I was pretty much convinced I was in for a dull life. I wasn't one of those slick types; you know the sort, always have a comment handy and know all the right things to say in any situation. And I didn't know the right people either, not like a well-connected successful person would. Basically you could say I was very much *disconnected* and on rare occasions when I opened my mouth in public I used to put at least one oversized foot directly into it.

"Well anyway, I was living in a tiny mining hamlet; you won't have heard of it and its gone now in any case, demolished, bulldozed, landscaped over. Life was a struggle; they were winding down the colliery so I had no job, no friends and all that. I only managed really thanks to the efforts of my poor old mam who worked double-shifts at the local abattoir and on Saturdays manned a stall at the market where she sold imaginative folk art welded together from pieces of industrial scrap.

"One day I was minding her stall, flicking through the classifieds in a well-thumbed copy of the Northumbrian Digest when I spotted a job ad that set my pulse racing:

Assistant Wanted!

Responsibilities:

General clerical duties and assistance in the field

Apply in writing to:

Professor Alexandra Terrine Claude-Spottelly.

Fearless Endeavours Ltd.

"Naturally I was very excited. At that time Professor Claude-Spottelly was a household name in the north of

England. A specialist in ancient history, she was one of those old world dilettante-types who dress in khaki, own bullwhips and have an amazing aura of mystery and adventure about them. In fact one of my most cherished possessions was a cracked tea mug with a fading black and white transfer of her opening the lost tomb of Coel Hen."

Peachy paused for breath, a faraway look coming into his eyes. Being very keen on punctuality I immediately took the opportunity to interrupt his rather rambling account.

"I'm sorry, Mr Peachy," I said, flicking a blonde curl out of my eyes, "but you really must get on. The museum closes in quarter of an hour and you've hardly even begun your tale."

"Wait just a darn minute, Gloria" he replied, frowning. "I've just noticed that you're speaking in the first person between items of direct speech; you shouldn't be doing that!"

I stared at him in silence. I didn't exactly understand what he meant but my confusion did nothing to lessen the moment's awkwardness. Then, after a little reflection I had the disturbing intimation of a vast hidden universe beyond the shallow strata of my world. Could this strange man view such secret dimensions as easily as I viewed his raggedy figure or the black iron scrollwork of the divan on which we were sitting?

"Erm, I shouldn't?"

"No, *I* should. *I'm* the one narrating the story!" Networks of spidery veins glowed red across his wrinkled cheeks and his grizzled brows were scrunched into a scowl.

"Well, erm, what ought I to be doing?"

"You should be in the third person for the most part and in the first person only when referring to yourself in direct speech!" he continued.

Even though I was completely out of my depth in philosophical matters of this kind I decided I needed to maintain an illusion of control. Having gained a diploma from the Open University in *Assertiveness Techniques for the Young and Inexperienced*, I knew that the only way forward was to tackle him head on.

"Nice try, Peachy, but you're actually only narrating *your* story to *me*. *I* on the other hand am narrating *the-story-of-how-you-narrated-your-story-to-me* to an invisible postulate, the reader. So you see, I simply *have to* use "I" in any meta-sequences that hold the other narrative passages together."

As per classic theory, I delivered my words gently, but firmly, hoping he would get on with things without growing any more irate.

Peachy was quiet for a bit, lips pursed. I sensed he wanted to argue, but was unable to decide if it were worthwhile or not. In the meantime all manner of thoughts were cascading through my head: *does the narrative still exist when the book is in the middle of a forest and nobody's there to read it; does the act of reading bring us into existence anew on each occasion in the alternate universes of each reader's mind, and what is the sound of one book cover clapping...*

At last Peachy reached a decision and a look of triumph crossed his face. He opened his mouth to speak, but at that precise moment an attendant walked by looking at his watch. Peachy glanced at him, shrugged and nodded. The triumphant expression was replaced with another that was significantly more contrite and the wind deserted his metaphorical sails.

"Time, pah! It's all an illusion, you know?" he muttered. "Yet without true consciousness we are temporal prisoners precisely as if it *were* real. Very well then, Gloria, we'll play things your way, but you might find you later change your mind about who is first and third person here!" And with that he got back to the telling while I breathed a silent sigh of relief.

"So, where was I? Ah yes, the job. I applied for it and got it, soon discovering that the Professor had a very specific task in mind for me hinted at in the line: *assistance in the field.*

"She was assembling a team of experts and specialists to investigate one of the greatest enigmas of northern Britain: the Spheres of Glammeth. You've heard of them of course?"

I shook my head.

"Ah, they teach young people nothing these days. You just wander around with heads full of poppycock and frivolous electronica. To be honest I hadn't heard very much about them back then either, but I was an under-privileged peon, so I'm excused. As I recall, the conversation between the Prof and I went something like this..."

At this point Peachy got up to perform the conversation. He played both roles by skipping lightly back and forth, calling out the name of the speaker in advance of each item of dialogue and changing the timbre and cadences of his voice to suit.

"Professor Claude-Spottelly: Long ago a being visited

our fair planet, a being from the outer reaches.

"Young Peachy: The outer reachers?

"Professor Claude-Spottelly: Those too.

"Young Peachy: What was it?

"Professor Claude-Spottelly: Nobody is certain. Some traditions speak of Glammeth, a malicious humanoid of vast size, others of various other fantastic interstellar creatures the like of which are beyond imagining.

"Young Peachy: And what happened to him...it, er, them?

"Professor Claude-Spottelly: Oh, the usual: he/it/they prowled the earth for a while, committing acts of horror and destruction. Then a hero emerged from an unexpected quarter to defeat it; or maybe the people of the world put aside their differences and united to bring it down; or perhaps it got the measles; or it might be that a daring and cocky young fellow flew some sort of flimsy fighter craft inside its defences and fired a couple of cheeky torpedoes into a gaping design flaw that led to its central nervous system...

"Young Peachy: Goodness! So many variations, but what do you think actually happened?

"Professor Claude-Spottelly: I really don't know. Whatever took place, the creature was laid low and the ensuing destruction was so great that the only thing left were its spheres.

"Young Peachy (sniggering): Spheres? Do you mean its...?!

"Professor Claude-Spottelly (sternly): Don't be childish, Peachy. Nobody knows for sure. All that we can be certain of is that we're dealing with two monstrous half-buried globes, ancient and unexplored.

"Young Peachy (contrite): Monstrous you say?

"Professor Claude-Spottelly: Yes, and fractal within. And that, not least, is what makes them special. Do you know what it means when such a thing goes fractal?

"Young Peachy: Can't say I do.

"Professor Claude-Spottelly: You're not alone in that! Among those of us who have an inkling there are fewer still who dare to dwell upon the implications. Of course they might not be its, you know, actual *balls!*

"Young Peachy (tiny chuckle): Well what then?

"Professor Claude-Spottelly: Who can say? Use your imagination. We might be dealing with the highest domes of a subterranean Camelot, parts of an ancient spacecraft or possibly even the forbidden egg-chambers of Zhogg.

"Young Peachy: Zhogg?

"Professor Claude-Spottelly (exasperated): Yes, *Zhogg!* Don't tell me you haven't heard of Zhogg!

"Young Peachy (lying): Oh you mean *Zhogg*, erm, yes of course.

"Professor Claude-Spotelly: Failing those possibilities the whole phenomenon might turn out to be an elaborate metaphysical metaphor, but if that's the case it will simply serve to deepen the mystery and increase their fascinatingly enigmatic significance."

His performance completed Peachy sat down next to me again. He was panting and a sheen of sweat glistened on his deeply lined forehead.

"The professor then went on to inform me what was actually known about them," he continued. "The spheres are two gigantic globes buried (but for a small exposed section) in the stony heather-clad loam of a wild and windswept Northumberland moor. It was her intention that we go to them, penetrate the outer shell and enter into the interior of the spheres to uncover their true nature."

At that precise moment a gong sounded and the attendant we'd seen earlier reappeared walking towards us. He said nothing merely tapping at his watch, a sympathetic expression on his face.

Peachy Gizzard And The Spheres Of Glammeth

"Oh blast, time's up!" Peachy cursed. "Here take these," he muttered opening his briefcase and thrusting a thick sheaf of grubby papers into my hands; then he got up and hurried off.

I glanced at his receding figure and subsequently began scanning the pages before me. It was with an inexplicable lurch of excitement that I realised we were already well-past the end of page three in his story and had actually made it all the way to the top of page five. A gut feeling seized me, not unlike aggravated dyspepsia; it brought with it the powerful sense that all hell was about to break loose!

Heart thudding I hurried through the cavernous building. I was suffering from light-headedness and the air seemed to thicken about me to a viscosity that made breathing a great labour. Perhaps it was a trick of the architecture, but the shadows appeared to bend and follow me, drawn to me in passing like iron filings to a magnet.

I speculated wildly that this might be some strange gravitational effect of Peachy's dimension-spanning manuscript. Little did I know...

At the main entrance I stopped dead, transfixed by something I'd never seen before in all my many visits to

the museum. Inscribed in the concrete lintel was a legend:
The Power of Three, The Unity of Four!

"Three and Four and I'm up to page five," I breathed.

As if by magic the attendant appeared.

"Madam, a parting thought on the nature of numbers and pages before you leave us. It is common editorial wisdom that an inexperienced writer will not infrequently start their short stories three or four pages too early."

"But I'm on page five," I blurted. "So that must mean..."

The attendant nodded and winked before ushering me out of the building: "That's right, madam," he called after me. "Whatever you do, hold onto your hat!"

His words left me even more perplexed. "I'm not wearing one," I murmured.

The plaza outside the museum was empty, the sky above grey. I waited for something exciting to occur. It didn't. I wandered to a nearby bus stop and sat down, puzzled and disappointed. Then my eyes strayed back to Peachy's dog-eared manuscript.

Aha! I thought and continued reading.

2. The Spheres of Glammeth

We tore across a shattered, wind-blasted landscape; triple diesel engines of the Bar-bhar-Mobile roaring, our course set for the Spheres of Glammeth. The other members of Professor Claude-Spotelly's illustrious team moved freely about the passenger area. Being the least experienced, however, I was strapped into my seat, helmet on, visor down.

Like a cross between a classic 65 litre Bentley and a Churchill infantry tank the Bar-bhar-Mobile seemed to owe as much of its robust frame to early motor car engineering as it did to the development of the mid-twentieth century AFV. But old-world styling can be deceptive and the multi-terrain vehicle enjoyed all the benefits of modernity. Solid titanium wheels with nineteen inch rubber quantum-pneumatic tyres thumped with ease over the broken land while the bodywork - a descendent of hyper-lightweight vehicle armours developed during the cold war at RARDE Chertsey - was both flexible and yet strong enough to take *almost* anything nature threw at it.

I have to admit to feeling rather peaky during the journey, but how could I confess such frailty to those around me? By comparison Professor Claude-Spotelly's team seemed so much at ease. Some chatted and laughed, drinking tea from enamelled metal mugs and exchanging anecdotes of expeditions gone by. Others struck heroic poses to stare with grim stoicism at the world whizzing past us.

Closest to me was A.C. McGrowther the fêted mountaineer and caver, known by some as the Bearded Fury of the Hills. He gazed stony-eyed and silent out at the landscape, a grease-proof paper package of his trademark cheese and soy-sauce sandwiches clutched in one hand. Beside him, dressed in a neoprene one-piece stood Ms Jay Wulfenstücke, a dark-haired, athletic woman in her mid-thirties. Wulfenstücke hailed from the village of Kill-Kreggan and was an internationally recognised authority on alien contact. I once asked her who Kreggan was and why the founding fathers of her village had wanted him dead. Her eyes lit up at my question and she confided she didn't know, but that finding the answer had become her life's work.

Next to her was perhaps the most mysterious member of the team: the scholar and mystic, Abdal Abu-Ur. Typically he was dressed in a bright turban, sumptuous khalat and pantaloons of blue silk. Known to most by his nickname *Baghdad Bill*, Abu-Ur was a self-professed Seeker of the Crossroads of Infinity. Throughout our journey he sat cross-legged on a large cushion, puffing on a foul-smelling hookah pipe. His eyes were mostly fixed on the middle-distance, though from time to time he would look up and say something inaudible to Ms Wulfenstücke, who invariably smiled at his comments.

In the cockpit, dressed in leathers, old-time flying helmets and aviation goggles, our erstwhile driver Renée Bar-bhar and her co-pilot Mrs Edith Balfour steered the Bar-bhar-Mobile with consummate skill. This wild duo hooted and howled with unbridled joy each time the vehicle crested a rise or leapt a gully and their silk scarves flowed in the wind behind them like banners.

After a particularly jarring series of bumps, I caught Professor Claude-Spotelly watching me. I was feeling somewhat unnerved at the time and her weathered features seemed to soften with affection. My heart leapt. I'd had a crush on her from the moment we'd first met and any hint that my infatuation might be reciprocated sent me into wild and blushing flights of fancy. Of course the more sober side of me knew that such a mature and distinguished paragon among women could not find anything to excite her in one so young and unaccomplished, but dreams have a life of their own and do not obey common logic.

"I say, aren't those the Spheres over there," Ms Wulfenstücke said pointing ahead to two perfect graphite mounds rising from the chaotic land.

"They are indeed!" screeched our driver. "Not long now, a minute or two only, and we'll be there."

The Professor smiled at me again and seemed just about to say something when with a thunderous rumbling a great pillar of rock thrust up from the heather directly ahead of us. Such was the unexpected suddenness of its appearance that not even Renée Bar-bhar could take evasive action in time. With a sickening crunch the Bar-bhar Mobile ploughed into the obelisk and the air resounded to the grind of tortured metal and crackle of splintering stone.

Less than a heartbeat after the impact we were high in the air, spinning over and over. At first I saw only ragged cloud and patches of blue sky, however, as the vehicle continued to gyrate through its complex trajectory I caught snatches of a curved grey surface. It was the closer of the two Spheres of Glammeth and we were arcing directly towards its dull apex!

The angle of our descent grew steeper and a terrifying howling, like that of a swarm of stukas, rose all around our toppling vehicle. Between spinning skies and whirling moors the great looming dome was coming closer. Thoughts sped through my mind like shoals of crazed fish. Our descent seemed to take an eternity, but sensing my time had come and that we were all to be dashed to pieces, I braced myself as best I might. Then there was a long deep, groaning sigh at which an eerie calm settled over me.

We came to a bone-jarring stop before rebounding, the super strong body of the vehicle twisting and buckling like a high-tech concertina. My battered frame was hurled and buffeted about, yet somehow the ultra-light harness held me in place, its multi-weave nano-fibre straps marking my pale flesh with plum-coloured stripes.

A human scream rose above the shriek of tearing metal and then a further nauseating impact was followed by silence.

I blacked out.

When I came to I was dangling by my harness, winded and giddy, swinging free of the titanium bucket seat in which I'd been ensconced. The tangled remains of the Bar-bhar Mobile were lying upside down on the sphere's fractured surface.

After a brief fumble, I managed to release the buckles and fell six feet to a twisted bulkhead, my body shuddering as pain vied with adrenalin for the upper hand.

"Professor!? Mr McGrowther? Ms Wulfenstücke?" I groaned, struggling to my feet and glancing about for signs that anyone else had survived.

A moan sounded from somewhere towards the front of the vehicle and I made my way towards it through a convoluted tunnel of wreckage. Clambering into an open area I recognised the remains of the vehicle's cockpit. Renée lay slumped over the dashboard, her leather flying helmet still in place, goggles spattered with oil and blood.

"Ms Bar-bhar, can you hear me?" I breathed.

She stirred, head flopping back, mouth hanging slack. "*Gerunds and infinitives*," she groaned.

"I'll see if I can find some of the others, I'll be right back," I promised making to leave, but she placed a hand on my arm and gave a weak shake of her head.

"No. It's too late for me. Please, hear my last confession."

"But I'm not a priest Ms Bar-bhar," I protested drawing back from her bloody hand.

"No matter, Peachy...I'm not actually religious...but I do have something to confess."

"It won't wait?" I wondered, hopefully.

She shook her head again.

"Okay then, I'm listening," I replied with more than a little trepidation.

"All my life...I've been a secret stickler for rules...directives...laws. Perhaps it's been some sort of compensation for all those wild adventures embarked upon in my role as a driver. Did you know for example..." She paused and a coughing fit seized her after which a thin trail of blood appeared at the corner of her mouth such as was often seen in Hollywood films of yesteryear. For a time she remained silent.

"Ms Bar-bhar?" I whispered, fearing she was gone.

Renée grunted, nodded and her lips parted. "Did you know that for years I have been moonlighting as a Specialist Grammar Consultant...though only at the weekends," she sighed.

I shook my head. "Truly I had no idea," I admitted.

"I operated under a pseudonym of course," she rattled.

"Of course," I agreed.

"But I have been *wrong*, Peachy. All my obsessions with prescriptive linguistics have blinded me to the true purpose of language..."

"I see," I said, not actually seeing in the slightest, but not knowing what else to say.

"Now that I am confronted with my impending demise, I realise what I should have known all along: form is *empty* in and of itself. The purpose of language is to convey a message...meaning is paramount in all things...regardless of form..." and then with a long groan she passed away, her fingers sliding from my arm.

Shaken by Renée's confession, but unable to grasp what she truly meant, I searched for the others. There was no trace of them in the vehicle.

Climbing out of the wreckage onto the smooth surface of the sphere I discovered the shattered body of Edith Balfour and beside her, strangely, Abdal Abu-Ur's hookah pipe. The pipe was upright, undamaged and still smouldering as if Abu-Ur had taken leave of it only moments earlier. Of Baghdad Bill himself there was no trace and in fact we never did discover what had happened to him. Experts have since put forward the theory that he opened a portal into another dimension just as the pillar rose to block our path. Perhaps they are right, but I doubt we'll ever know for sure.

Some distance beyond the pipe a ragged hole gaped in the otherwise perfect surface of the sphere. The rupture had almost certainly been caused by our initial impact after which, I conjectured, the Bar-bhar Mobile had rebounded and caromed to its final resting position.

Contemplation of the dark aperture unnerved me and I was steeling myself to look into its inky depths when a hand appeared on the shattered lip followed by the bruised but stern visage of AC McGrowther.

"What're ye doing lallying aboot oot here? Ferfugzake Peachy, get yoursel' over here, man!"

I was startled and outraged at his tone. Part of me wanted to tell him where to go, but there's an air of command about McGrowther in situations like this that quite frankly brooks no argument.

"What on earth are you doing in there?" I asked rather weakly instead.

"Am looking fer you, what d'ya suppose am doin'? The Professor went an' fell through the hole when we crashed. She's hurt. Wulfenstücke's doon there with her noo."

McGrowther had climbed up to the lip using his mountaineering prowess along with a few ropes. But how would I manage who suffered from vertigo when climbing out of the bath? I sat on the edge of the hole, sweating and dizzy. Inside the sphere a labyrinth of tunnels and chambers stretched away into the gloom.

"C'moan noo, get yersel' roped up and let's get doon there to see what the Professor wants to do aboot things!"

Very much against my better judgement I complied with McGrowther's instructions and moments later I was descending into the weird inner world of the Sphere.

It seemed that our crash had not only holed the outer shell of the sphere, but opened a fissure that led through its weirdly convoluted interior. Everywhere the grey walls and surfaces self-illuminated by means of some microscopic light emitting cells; a luminous fungal growth perhaps.

After what felt like an age of sweaty palms and rope burns we arrived in a chamber shaped like a dodecahedron on the floor of which lay the Professor, attended to by Ms Wulfenstücke.

"Oh, Peachy, you survived," the Professor croaked in a weak voice. "Come closer my boy. The responsibility for the success of my mission rests now upon your young shoulders."

McGrowther gave a throaty "Harrumph!" clearly not happy with this latest piece of news.

"But Professor," I replied, both puzzled and afraid. "I don't know the first thing to do."

Peachy Gizzard And The Spheres Of Glammeth

"We all start that way my boy," she said, taking my hand.

I gazed into her face, paler than ever, deeply lined beneath her thickly applied white foundation and dusting of scarlet rouge. A tremor passed through her body, her mouth trembled and the wiry hairs on her top lip quivered.

"There isn't much time, Peachy. Listen carefully..."

"Oh no, you're not going to start rambling on about grammar and stuff like Renée are you? I couldn't stand that, really I couldn't," I bleated, tears in my eyes.

"What on earth are you talking about? I thought I told you to *listen*," the Professor snapped, a note of familiar irritation creeping into her voice.

"Sorry," I replied, heartened by her return to irascible form.

"Peachy, these Spheres have been here since ancient times. Longer even. Whatever really put them onto our earth did so at a point lost in the mists of prehistory. Yet despite that, nobody has yet subjected them to serious examination. Why do you suppose that is?"

"Well, I don't really know, I..."

"My question was rhetorical; be *quiet* and *listen!*"

"Sorry."

"My theory is that people over the ages have been confounded by their innate strangeness; their perfection. Look at them when you are next outside, they are the very antithesis of natural form; so smooth, so uniform in pigmentation, so unerringly spherical.

"However, I have long suspected that their perfection is a ruse to distract the observer from their true value: that which lies within. It is my belief, dear Peachy, that the Spheres hide a great secret."

I nodded enthusiastically, but kept quiet, not wishing to awaken her ire again.

"Well, aren't you going to *say* anything?" she growled.

"Erm, you're bound to be right Professor. I guess."

The Professor sighed and shook her head. "Recently I discovered a fragment of an ancient text attributed to the writer and magician Zosimos. In it he mentions the Spheres and how in the course of a series of visions a man of metal told him that in their heart lies a great arcanum guarded by a terrifying guardian."

"Terrifying?" I echoed, my mouth going dry.

The Professor nodded, her eyes glinting. "Find it, Peachy. Make me proud! Go into the heart of the Sphere and uncover the secret." She exhaled deeply and closed her eyes. Her breathing had become so shallow that I thought she'd died and tears splashed down my cheeks.

Moved by the solemnity of the moment I placed my right hand over my heart and said:

"Professor, I swear I'll do this for you and the betterment of humankind; failing that I shall perish in the attempt!"

Her eyes fluttered open briefly, thin lips curling into a weak smile. "Oh Peachy just look at you; you're so young and strong in spirit and body. If only we'd had more time: I would have loved you like a son...or something." And at that she breathed her last.

"Reet, well that's me oot a here. Ahm nay hangin aboot to be led to ma doom by a glaikit wee boy," McGrowther announced. "What aboot you Wulfenstücke: are you coming?"

Ms Wulfenstücke shook her head, "Not for a while yet. Now that we're here we might as well explore a little and see what we can find out about the Spheres, don't you think?"

I flashed her a grateful smile. But McGrowther just shook his head.

"Och away with yous. I'm nay stayin'!" and with that he began climbing back up the ropes and out of the Sphere.

"Come on, Peachy, never mind him," Wulfenstücke said taking my hand. "I was growing tired of his grumbling anyway. Look, there's a tunnel over there. Let's see where it leads."

And so we set off together into the gloomy half-light of a hexagonal corridor and while I truly wanted to make good my promise to the Professor, each step in that place eroded my already fragile courage. Perhaps Ms Wulfenstücke sensed this for she gave my hand a squeeze and flashed me one her rather lovely smiles.

"Be brave, sweet boy. Together we must deeply examine and explore these passages," she said, her eyes glittering.

Her choice of words struck me as curious and their effect on me was both profound and some might say, unsavoury. Shaped by the delayed effects of shock, the perceived proximity to danger and perhaps some darker force emanating from deep within the Sphere, my retort was both brazen and bold.

"I'd feel braver exploring your passages for a while Ms W," I breathed, my voice little more than a husky whisper.

"*Peachy!*" she cried with shock that I earnestly hoped was feigned. My face crimson and mouth dry I squirmed with embarrassment, assuming I'd gone too far. But then she winked at me, her customary smile broader than ever.

Peachy Gizzard And The Spheres Of Glammeth

"Well then young man, if we're really going to screw your courage to the sticking place, we'd better do something about these desires of yours first," she suggested, her manner now sly and teasing.

I nodded, growing giddy with anticipation as she unzipped the crotch section of her neoprene suit to reveal the perfect curves of her womanhood.

"How should we go about this then?" she inquired softly.

"From behind, against the wall!" came my hoarse reply, every adolescent fantasy I'd ever entertained as an unemployed northerner coming home to roost.

"Yes," she hissed, "I'd like that!" and she turned about, presenting her perfect rear to me. The physical part of what happened next is indistinct in my mind, though the memory of my feelings remains strong and clear. I recall descending on her like hawk, my stiff member sliding easily into her welcoming body. We coupled wildly and passionately, she singing sea shanties as I thrust in and out, and then, after a blissful, timeless age, we slammed our bodies together in a shuddering climax. For a few seconds it felt as if we had fused, becoming one flesh. Then the rush of our ardour faded and we peeled ourselves into separation again.

I recall that we regarded each other, gazes locked. I felt weak, weary, yet content; reduced and yet increased. I stood revealed to myself: a mortal creature of the flesh, a passing blip in the annals of eternity. Yet robbed of all delusion, pretence and bluster I was tempered by the knowledge of my insignificance and had become the greater for it.

I couldn't be sure if she felt the same way, but her lovely face was flushed and if she appeared drained she was also visibly happy. She made me promise that we'd do it again a bit later and try a few other positions she was fond of, all of which I took as a promising sign.

Taking my hand again she led me further into the corridor, glancing at me often with that smile of hers. As no doubt was her purpose I was happily encouraged by her continued attentions, though from time to time I did detect a trace of melancholy about her eyes that spawned some niggling worm of unease in my heart of hearts.

The hours wore on. We traversed both great halls and winding passages all illuminated in the same dull shades of grey. There were long convoluted sequences of multi-facetted space, fantastical in form, yet soulless and plain in aspect. The more complex spaces were often interconnected by short sections of tunnel, which reminded me of grey ceramic drainage pipes. We were forced to pass through these on our hands and knees, blistering our palms and often banging our heads in the process.

Then we came to the great chasm. Stumbling out from a lengthy section of crooked corridor we arrived at a broad platform of polished stone. There were no walls here, only the all-enveloping vastness of night. The path beyond the platform was along a narrow way, scarcely a yard wide and completely exposed on every side. Ms Wulfenstücke and I exchanged glances and for the first time I detected a hint of fear in those intelligent eyes.

We stopped then, unable to force ourselves to continue and neither daring to speak, as if the presence of the void had rendered us mute. Instead we communicated by means of shrugs and facial expressions, mouthing silent words and indicating the path ahead with hand gestures. The gist of our exchange boiled down to: *Should we press on or would it be better to retrace our steps?*

I contemplated the pale exposed strip at length; the path was straight, running like a lance through darkness. It wasn't so very narrow, surely we could make it across? But doubts crowded in, dulling my mind and I could not decide.

This creeping despondency seemed to settle over us both and we turned from one another, lost in the troubled ruminations of our personal inner realms. How long had we already wandered in the strange milieu of Glammeth's Sphere? Hours or days; I no longer knew. From dark inner oceans that perfectly mirrored those without a voice whispered to me to turn back. Yet beneath the shackles of sluggish mind another voice was calling to me: *Press onward, Peachy! Find your destiny!*

Looking up I found Ms Wulfenstücke watching me. Instinctively, I realised that she had come to her conclusion – *onward* – and it was her silent resolve that tipped the scales for me. Smiling again she pointed to the mouth of the corridor behind us and with a series of winks and lewd gestures suggested that it might be an idea for us to make love again before setting off over the chasm.

Her proposal caught me unprepared and at first I didn't respond. Perhaps she took this reticence for unwillingness for she continued to lobby for her proposal with increasingly expressive body language:

Peachy we really should do this in order to steel ourselves! – she seemed to be saying. *And given the likely arduous nature of the trials ahead, I think we ought to*

Peachy Gizzard And The Spheres Of Glammeth

invest unreserved gusto and inventiveness in our love-play — she then appeared to add.

Who am I to argue with you, I gesticulated, rounding off my sign-language tirade with a literal bow to her wisdom.

Never since have I experienced the equal of that which followed. Afterwards, a little sore here and there, but warmed by a fierce inner glow, we stepped out onto the luminous gangway. Almost at once everything changed.

Within moments the platform we had so recently departed was lost to sight. It seemed to me that it had been physically removed or perhaps that we'd been metaphysically transported to another place.

We trudged on along an endless path through timeless night, forced to keep to single file by dread darkness and the peril of the abyss. For a very long time we neither spoke nor signalled, then we heard the Guardian call.

The first I felt was a vibration so slight and dubious that I believed it a trembling palsy in the soles of my feet brought on by fatigue. Soon, however, waves of infrasound rolled through the chill air followed by the low rumbling roar of the beast as it impressed itself on our senses and gathered strength in the manner of an approaching storm.

As the crescendo peaked the very darkness pulsed and the din formed so great an assault upon us that neither Wulfenstücke nor I could keep our feet. We lay instead huddled in one another's' arms, babes before a cosmic terror. And then just as I was sure we would be obliterated, the crashing roar ceased and silence rushed in, like a balm to our ringing ears.

How long we remained there in blissful, wordless embrace I cannot judge; a day, perhaps a week. All I know is that the comfort our proximity bestowed on us was greater than that of all our lovemaking combined. We stayed thus until the boundaries between us had faded and I was no longer certain where I ended and she began. Then we rose, exchanged meaningful glances and silent nods and pressed on as we both knew we must.

Shortly beyond that point we reached the far side of the chasm; the exposed pathway coming to an end without drama or fanfare.

We found ourselves in a spacious passage carved from limestone by unnatural processes. The contrast with both chasm and the dull passages before it could not have been greater: braziers and pine torches sputtered and flared from rusting brackets and sconces; rock crystal, agate and topaz glittered from the walls in dazzling clusters that both magnified and refracted the flickering light.

As if a weight had been lifted from us, we both breathed more easily and began to speak again. Wulfenstücke's soft laughter tinkled like music, blending with the haze of colour and brilliance and she hummed those beloved sea shanties of hers.

We wandered onward until she stopped, the smile fading from her lips.

"What's that?" she murmured, pointing ahead.

Some tens of metres before us a curious silver object was suspended at waist height above the floor of the tunnel; it was rotating slowly about the vertical axis. Long and angular with various appendages and outcroppings it appeared to be some fanciful form of firearm.

"I don't know, Wolfy," I admitted.

As we drew closer it became clear that the object was indeed intended to symbolise a weapon. However, at our approach, its outline grew increasingly jagged, the surface pixelating until all detail was lost.

"Look, there on the floor beside it," Wulfenstücke said pointing to the crude representation of a helmet with some sort of flashing screen attached where one might expect a visor to be.

"You know, I don't think these objects are really here," I commented. "I mean I know we can see them, but I think they're some sort of projection without any physical substance."

I moved toward the helmet and reached for it. As I'd suspected my hands met empty air where the helmet should have been. At the same time, however, a most peculiar change came over me.

"Wolfy, something's happened to my vision," I gasped.

"Peachy, the helmet's disappeared...wait a minute you're *wearing* it!" she squeaked.

I reached up and found that my head was completely encased in some sort of hard, lightweight material. But that wasn't the strangest thing. Superimposed over my view of the tunnel was a heads-up display that would have made a fighter pilot proud. An information bar running along the lower edge of my field of vision included a series of stats and an icon that resembled an animated passport photo of myself.

"What do you see, Peachy?" Wulfenstücke asked, breathlessly.

"Ammo 00; Health 100%; Weapons...I don't actually have any weapons; Armor 0%."

"You can see all that?" she continued intrigued.

Peachy Gizzard And The Spheres Of Glammeth

"Yes, it's sort of written across the bottom of my eyes; don't ask how."

"Walk into the twirling gun thingy and see what happens then," she urged.

I did so and as if by magic the weapon appeared in my hands. No longer crudely realised it was now every bit as solid and well-defined as the rock beneath my feet. A line of text flashed in the upper left of my vision.

"You've got the hypergun!!!" I read aloud.

"The *hypergun?*" she echoed.

"Yes. Ammo: 150 rounds."

If I was confounded by this latest strange series of events I was to be even more perturbed when I decided to sling the weapon over my shoulder. To my horror I found I couldn't put it down; it was fused to my flesh.

"Try removing the helmet," Wulfenstücke suggested. But that didn't help either because I couldn't grip anything with my hands full of the hypergun.

"Can you do it for me?" I asked her.

Wulfenstücke set to with a will until, yelping with pain, I begged her to stop.

"It won't budge," she admitted grimly.

"I think I'm stuck like this," I moaned. "And that means I won't be able to touch you again."

"I'm afraid you're right, for now at least," she agreed.

With heavy hearts we trudged on like two weary snails, time trickling by at a pace to match. Around us the glittering tunnel continued with little variation, an endless series of pine torches, braziers and crystal prisms. That which had been so lovely after the horrors of the chasm now struck me as depressingly monotonous.

We wandered ever further until I detected the first hints of a certain unsavoury quality to the air. Torches and braziers were becoming less frequent and leaping shadows gradually replaced the dazzle and glitter.

As the rank undertone grew more noticeable Wulfenstücke detected it too. "Something foul lies ahead," she offered.

"Something dead more like," I muttered and raised the hypergun in readiness for trouble.

Shortly thereafter Wulfenstücke stopped in her tracks and grabbed my arm. "Look there Peachy, someone's sitting by that pile of rocks!"

I squinted into the gloom and saw that she was right; the woman had damned good eyes.

"Hello; who goes there?" I called waving my hypergun in what I hoped was a menacing fashion. But whoever it was showed no sign they'd heard us. As we drew nearer we realised why: the man, a dwarf adventurer by the look of his ruined gear and long wispy beard, had been dead for at least six months. Seated at the base of a pile of shattered stone his mouldering skull sagged forward onto a sunken chest. His garments, once fine in a dwarfly way, were black with blood. His gear lay scattered around him.

Eyes watering from the foul air, I looked away.

"Wish I could drop this stupid gun and put a hand over my nose to shut out the stench," I complained.

A crude wooden signpost had been driven into the pile of rocks behind our deceased friend, but of the sign itself there was no trace.

"Look you can see here were the nails have been ripped out of the post," Wulfenstücke said, tracing the splintered wood with her fingers. "I wonder what it said."

"Looks like it was removed with some violence," I replied in a quiet voice.

Beyond the rocks lay the carcass of a pack mule, badly savaged by some form of carrion-eaters and beyond that the tunnel forked into two darkened passages, both of which led off in opposite directions.

"What now?" I wondered, sinking onto my haunches. But the air was worse closer to the ground and gagging on the stink, I struggled upright again.

"Look, Peachy!" Wulfenstücke shouted. "He scratched a message into the floor of the tunnel before he died."

Those sharp eyes of hers again!

Clasped in his rotting right hand the dwarf still held a piece of limestone used to carve his dying message.

"There's an arrow here pointing to the right-hand passage and some words," Wulfenstücke continued. "I can't quite make them out though; something about a secret, I think. Yes: *That way lies the secret.*"

"What about those marks over there?" I wondered pointing at another sequence of crudely scratched hieroglyphs. "I suppose they say where the other passage leads."

Wulfenstücke crouched by the second string of characters and at once became very still and quiet.

"This is it," she gasped, her voice tremulous. "It's the way to *Kreggan's doom!*"

"Kreggan? You mean? Are you *sure?*" I wondered, growing alarmed at the change in her. Squinting at the writing over her shoulder I shook my head. "That doesn't say Kreggan...looks more like Kaggan to me, or maybe even *Keegan.*"

Peachy Gizzard And The Spheres Of Glammeth

"No Peachy," she said in a voice husky with emotion. "It's definitely Kreggan. I've been searching for this all my life; the answer to the riddle of Kill-Kreggan."

"Alright then, we'll go that way when we've uncovered the other secret, the big one..." I began.

"No, no. I can't. My path lies down the left-hand tunnel. Sorry lover, but unless you're coming with me to Kreggan's doom, this is where we part company, at least for a while."

"But you can't be serious! Have you forgotten your promise to the Professor?" I protested.

"*I* made no promises Peachy; that was you! Go ahead, find the secret of the Spheres of Glammeth; it is your path. I, however, have to follow my own destiny, though with luck we'll meet again soon enough."

I pleaded, reasoned, appealed to her better nature and even her mothering instincts; the last of which did little to impress her. However, her mind was made up. I toyed briefly with the idea of following her, but much as a strong sense of destiny compelled me to pursue the Secret of the Spheres, another even stronger foreboding told me that the left-hand tunnel was a path of no return.

"Please don't go that way, Wulfy," I begged. "I have a really bad feeling about it and I'd hate for anything to happen to you."

Wulfenstücke's eyes moistened and she approached me, her hand caressing the side of my carbotanium shielded head.

"Oh Peachy, you sweet, sweet boy," she sighed. "If only we could get you out of that helmet I'd kiss you and if only you weren't strangely fused to that monstrous hypergun I'd take your hands in mine. But sometimes fate decrees that two people must be separated, even when the strongest feelings cause them by nature to gravitate together.

"We are adventurers you and I, danger is an integral part of our lives; the stakes are high, but the rewards are all the greater as a result. We have to be true to ourselves and follow the strands of fate that draw us into their weave. Then, when we have done that which we must, and if destiny will have it, we shall once more find solace in one another's arms."

So saying she gave me a peck on the helmet and marched off down the left-hand tunnel where she was soon swallowed by shadow.

At once everything was different. Had she been holding back the sheer terror of Glammeth by her presence alone?

Peachy Gizzard And The Spheres Of Glammeth

The air around me became a chill void and dread rushed in like dark tidal waters, swirling in frothing torrents and coursing on through all the myriad tunnels and passages of that horrid place.

In my insignificance I was anchored to that lonely spot, nothing to keep me from drowning in the vortex of fear but some stubborn nub of courage that might at any moment wear away and leave me at the mercy of madness.

Onwards is your path, Peacham Gizzard. You must *go on!* A voice whispered from the shadows. Whose had it been? The Professor's or some other shadowy force.

No! I cried.

Face your destiny, Peachy! The voice called again.

I cannot!

You must! It insisted.

I will not!

My eyes strayed to the corpses, contemplating their ruined flesh as a means of evading that which I could not face. The pressure grew and still I struggled, but procrastination could not hold out in the face of a destiny which would not be refused.

No! I declared a final time, eyes stinging, skin prickling and burning.

Oh dammit, very well then!

I glanced up and away from the corpses, away from the left-hand tunnel and straight into the dark aperture of the one on the right; *my* tunnel.

I was chanceless once more. That blackness was a wall, penetrable to some, but not I. And such little resolve as I'd mustered drew back again, every timorous heartbeat another retreat.

Cannot!

Maybe I could go back...? But a single glance stolen over the Devil's shoulder told me that a return the way we'd come was equally impossible; I simply lacked the energy to stumble and traipse all that long weary way.

Can't go on, can't go back. In that case I'm staying here! I cried.

If that is your decision you leave me no choice, the tunnels seemed to sigh.

That was when I heard her first scream. Piercing and shrill the cry was followed by a brief span of silence. Another more protracted wail followed on, cutting me to the core. That second wordless utterance contained such an intensity of despair and pain that my knees gave way and I fell forward.

"Wulfy, oh *Wulfy!*" I sobbed. For instinctively I knew we would never hold one another again.

Peachy Gizzard And The Spheres Of Glammeth

One final time she cried out in a shriek that was cut off almost as soon as it began. Then the air was full of the sound of many feet pattering along the stone floors towards me.

Quaking with dread I struggled into a kneeling position, hypergun up at the ready.

Ammo: 150, the heads-up display flashed.

Was that really all? 150 sounded so very little all of a sudden.

They emerged from the dark: short, squat, roughly humanoid, their thick, stubby limbs like pistons as they sprinted towards me. Massive hands with gleaming sabre-claws flailed the air. Their outsized eyeless heads were conical and hirsute, a dozen fleshy appendages writhing around their pointed snouts, as if they were some species of giant star-nosed mole.

I fired without thinking, depressing the trigger for no more than a few heartbeats. The gun spewed out hissing orange streaks that lit the tunnels in hot pulses and crackled and sputtered when they met flesh. There were no cries, the mole-men simply disintegrated into smouldering chunks, thudding and bouncing along the tunnel floor toward me.

Peachy Gizzard And The Spheres Of Glammeth

I swallowed. The tunnel was clear but a thousand footfalls still pattered from the dark.

Ammo: 96.

How could I have used so many rounds so quickly? I had to focus more; controlled bursts were the only way. Other mole-men appeared. I pressed lightly on the trigger for a fraction of a second. Pulses ripped from the hypergun in twos and threes, each energy bolt tearing into and through a half dozen of the beasts.

Ammo: 92...90...89...86...82...

Better! But still too many rounds too quickly...

The press was such that they were closing in faster than I could take them down. The frontrunners only yards distant, were drawing back those lethal hands to rend me with their talons. Unless I acted I would be theirs at any moment.

"For *Wolfy* and the *Prof.*" I screamed, getting to my feet and letting them have it.

After six seconds the hypergun coughed, clucked and jerked. Magazines empty, it fell from my trembling hands to clatter on the rock floor. A numbness spread over me; I'd gone beyond saturation point and something new and grim was overriding the fear that had been crippling me.

Peacham Gizzard, you must go on! – the voices insisted.

The left-hand tunnel was choked with smoking carnage. Perforated bodies smouldered and steamed; small fires sizzled in pools of molten fat. I drew in a deep breath, the hot air heavy with the odour of charred mole-man.

My fear was gone and in its place icy rage had gripped me.

Taking up a notched sword from beside the dead mule, I pondered briefly how a warrior of dwarfly stature could ever have wielded such a long and heavy weapon. It was almost too much for me. Soon, however, all such considerations faded and striding toward the right-hand tunnel, and my destiny, I dared the dark to do its worst.

3. The Guardian

Numb, grim determined, I walked through the murk, my powerful strides the wiry spring of enraged youth. Undaunted, uncaring and now wholly unafraid my eyes scanned the impenetrable shadows, focused by fury, fierce and unflinching. A song writhed from within me, a chant without melody, its beat the stomping of feet, the gnashing of teeth, the tearing of hair, the clashing of spear on shield rim.

Peachy Gizzard And The Spheres Of Glammeth

The old crone is dead,
My wolf-lover slain,
This curséd place the cause!
    I will slay you Guardian!
        Carve you asunder,
        Unman you with my blade,
        Cut out your liver,
        Flay you for a cloak,
        Feast on your eyes,
        Dine on your sweetbreads!
I am the blade that will bring about your fall!
My sword the heirloom of a dwarfish house,
Craves vengeance for its master's doom,
And I shall grant it the just outcome,
Settling thereby all accounts,
I will slay you Guardian!
The old crone is dead
My wolf-lover is slain,
This curséd place the cause!
    As surely as my song repeats,
    Each nested loop programs me:
    Body and Mind;
    Body and Soul;
    Body and Spirit

ANDREW COULTHARD

And so my anthem cycles,
Building courage from wrath,
One-pointed, I am the vengeful blade!

I sang until I grew hoarse and my parched throat and tongue were become cracked leather. And when I could sing no more my battle-rage pulsed to the drumming of my feet against rock. Together they beat out a war dirge, the funeral song of the *Guardian.*

And then a fierce spark appeared in the benighted tunnel, resolving itself into a distant hoop of bright flame. A portal, it was, ringed about with flickering tongues of yellow heat and carved from porphyry to mimic a magic mouth agape. And in my steely heart instinct whispered that I stood before the gateway to the Guardian's Hall.

Caution slowed me then. From the words of the Wise One it is widely known that before one can wend through a doorway one must look about; it is ever uncertain where foes and fiends might lay in wait. And so I adopted wariness, stealing forward, cloaked in darkness, my martial tramp replaced by surreptitious steps.

And passing through the blazing gate I entered a vast cavern, dimly lit by faint light that came from a pulsing fleshy mountain at its heart. I paused to let my eyes adjust to the gloom, for they'd been dazzled by the flickering portal now behind me.

I discovered that the path stopped short, mere feet beyond the portal. A thin ledge no more than a stone strip was all there was and beyond that a huge drop into the cavern's giddying expanses.

The fleshy mountain stirred and though distant, I estimated it to be perhaps three hundred feet high and a quarter mile about. Dark forms, indistinct and massive as tower blocks unfurled across its surface. The light, a dim and sickly glow, was issuing from whatever lay beneath these terrible silhouettes.

And so my newfound courage met its first true test. Was *this* the Guardian? How could I, Peacham Aglaeca Gizzard, pit myself against a living mountain? I couldn't even get down to the thing.

But then I spied a most curious craft. It was tethered by a ragged hawser at the furthest extreme of the little ledge on which I stood. A boat not more than twelve feet long, low of prow, high of stern. It bobbed gently as if riding at anchor, yet floated, in truth, on the air of the cavern. The prow was carved to resemble a graceful beast; a cross between a dragon and a horse. The high stern formed the dragon-steed's sturdy tail, curled and ornamented as befitted such an artefact of myth and magic.

How should I propel and steer this strange vehicle and more to the point, how would I tackle the enigmatic monstrosity that awaited me below? I could not know. All I was certain of was that the boat was awaiting *me* and thither lay my path.

Hefting the dwarfish blade I stepped from the rock onto the narrow deck of seasoned oak. At once I was instilled with a sense of solidity and dependability. The vessel bobbed and rocked just as it would if resting on calm waters, but my feet seemed to grip the planks and were firm.

Gazing out across the dingy vastness, I wished silently that we could sail high over the writhing leviathan that I might spy out its extent from directly above. The boat jerked at once, straining at the mooring rope, able to read my thoughts and eager, it seemed, to do my bidding. As it shuddered and wrenched I almost lost my footing and fell overboard.

Avast there! I bid the curious craft with thought alone and it ceased its struggles in the very same instant. I untied the rope and clung to the gunwales, making my way back to centre deck where I braced my feet in the stance of a champion boarder. *Now take me where I wanted*, I commanded and we shot off across the darkness, sailing as silent and true as a spear cast.

Hundreds of feet below me, beams of morbid light lanced out, piercing the gloom like searchlights. The mountain was erupting; dark forms I'd previously spied now uncoiling into colossal limbs as thick as five men and lengthy enough to reach from floor to ceiling.

They snaked upwards, lunging at me with awe-inspiring speed and power. My vessel pitched and rolled out of their reach while I was afforded glimpses of their weird composition. Like animated totem poles they were formed from stacks of demon faces fused within a vast muscular chord. Their oily, bloated flesh dripped discharge and stank of corpses.

I willed my craft to avoidance and brandished the sword. With swift compliance the magic vessel wove dexterous portraits of complexity on the air, flitting between swooping and snapping jaws. Scores of hateful eyes swivelled in pursuit of me; be-fanged orifices emitted thunderous roars and piercing siren wails. Theses flexing columns of tightly-stacked ettin laboured as one to bring about my destruction.

Now that each murky demon-member was in action, the glowing mountain at their root lay fully revealed. What met my gaze as I glanced down was a scabrous and suppurating human head of colossal size. Eyes closed, face downcast, the visage was the very picture of pain and suffering. Could these writhing columns, protruding from its ulcerated flesh, be some form of rabid parasite?

Dragon-steed, brine-stallion of the air; take me closer still that I may strike at these foul demons, but do all in your power to keep me beyond their wrathful reach!

The vessel responded on the instant, weaving and swooping among them so close that sometimes there was no more than a hair's breadth to spare. Time after time I swung the long-sword, feeling wild exultation as its ancient edge bit into their toxic flesh.

I kept my balance and my arm stayed strong; soon their bellowing changed its pitch from fury to alarm. Like a flickering sting, my sword was slicing long slits into their foul flesh which shortly gaped wide. Behind me, yellow putrescence stained the air, jetting from yawning gashes and crossing itself in steaming trails.

How long we fought I cannot say. Body, blade and indeed boat became as one. An impulse no sooner born was translated into action: swish, thud, and the tentacles bemoaned their agony. But I did not rest on these little victories; instead I sliced them again and again with tireless resolve. And then as I at last began to wonder how much longer my vengeance-fuelled strength could prevail, one of them fell.

The beast was swiping at me, engaging us both in the aerial dance. I met its gloating visage full on with a blow that jarred my arm; soundless it vanished from sight. I glanced over the gunwale in time to see its collapsing form crash about the glowing head in bursting ruin. My heart leapt and my knotted body regained anew the strength and quality of spring steel. I'd hardly dared to believe I would prevail, but now I knew they could be killed.

The next followed its mate soon after and then another and another, until at last only one, the largest and most ferocious, still remained.

The arena was calmer now; the fetid cavern air no longer full of writhing peril. My boat and I had little difficulty in avoiding the attentions of the final monstrous column of flesh, yet something about this one impressed me as different. An insane conglomerate of scales and animal features, it seemed to hold the hint of a secret form at a point where porcine, bovine and reptilian elements combined like some mad god's fancy. As I circled, I recognised the hidden shape to be an approximation of a Human embryo, though at ten yards high it could never have been birthed by mortal woman.

"What now?" I wondered aloud.

The vast pillar turned in my direction and a great tusked snout at its crown spoke to me:

"What indeed? My guess would be that you will make quick work of me as you have these others and then descend upon the well-spring from which we flow."

The words floating across the cavern were both intelligent and sorrowful, seemingly born on a flow of melodic cadences that had a strangely soothing effect upon me.

"What would you have me do otherwise?" I asked, curious about its thinking and glad of an opportunity to rest my sword arm.

"I have no will in the matter. We are what we are, creations of a primordial force, and we act not through whim, caprice or any other conscious form of volition, but according to our nature."

Are we coming a little closer to one another while we speak? I wondered, peering at the bizarre monster. *Or is it just some weird trick of the gloom?*

Peachy Gizzard And The Spheres Of Glammeth

Despite a growing tingle of unease, I found that my curiosity was piqued; I simply couldn't resist continued interaction.

"Why are you different from the others and what of that child-shape inside you?" I asked.

"The Guardian's soul is ailing. This vast realm is formed of the stuff of his mind; I too am made of that very material, as are the many others who you have not yet met. Those you slew, however, where more a symptom of his illness or indeed, a manifestation of its causes."

I glanced down at the nightmarish mounds of broken bone and tissue below.

"Then I have not hurt the Guardian, I have excised his disease," I mumbled in dismay.

"In a manner of speaking, you have performed a perfect psychosisectomy."

My shoulders slumped. All that struggle and my only accomplishment was to make the Guardian stronger.

"And the child?" I continued as an afterthought.

"I am not aware of the child of which you speak!" This time the creature's words were delivered in a thunderous bellow that struck me like a shockwave and reverberated about the cavern, and at last I woke to danger. During our exchange the monstrosity had reeled me in as a fisherman his unwary catch. Without knowing how, I was now mere yards from the colossal boar-tusked snout. At its very apex, what I'd previously assumed to be horny growth revealed itself to be the wizened corpse of a wise-man in shrivelled lotus position.

There was no time for reflection on what this might mean, the beast's maw was gaping wide and lunging for me, its intent clear enough. I willed the boat on a radical course that I did not become fully conscious of until we had followed it halfway through.

It swept sharply upward, cheating the clamping jaws; though the beast snapped off a section of the carven stern despite our fleetness. I then spun us over in a loop so tight that centrifugal forces kept me pinned to the deck. Down we plunged after that, straight at the monster. My blade before me, I leapt ahead, the very glittering point impacting with the scaly carapace of its forehead.

There was a clap of thunder and the beast split in two, its monstrous hide separating into neat, equal halves and peeling away from the giant infant at its core.

I hovered before the iridescent babe, patterns swirling across its skin, eyes blinking from every inch of its body.

The wise man drifted down to the babe in a sluggish yet graceful arc. He had lost his desiccated look and in place of grey parchment qualities, his skin had now acquired a healthy bloom. Still in perfect lotus pose he landed at the nameless spot dead centre of the infant's head. At once his eyes opened.

"So, you see beyond apparent forms to that which lies at the heart of the matter, young warrior?" he said.

"I saw this strange babe within the conglomerate monster, if that is your meaning," I confirmed.

He nodded. "And what will you do now? Slay me? Slay the babe?"

I looked from one to the other. "To tell the truth I would prefer to slay neither of you. My business was with the Guardian. Its defences on the moors caused the death of my friends and after that, a horde of rabid mole-men took the life of my lover."

"Do you not seek the secret of the Spheres of Glammeth?" the wise man asked surprised. "If you kill our friend below then there will be none to reveal it."

"I am not sure I care about the secret any longer. That was actually the Professor's dream."

"Yet you promised her," the wise man chided.

"Perhaps, but I have changed so much in my short time down here that I dare to say it was another, former, self who promised her that service. I am no longer the boy who stumbled into this madness."

The wise man nodded. "Very well, make your choice; have at us or grant us mercy."

I did not trust the wise man, far less the weird infant floating like a psychedelic blimp before me. Yet the battle lust had faded in me. "Mercy it is," I replied curtly.

"Then you shall have your audience with the Guardian," the wise man replied and together they descended to the tortured head and vanished into a gaping orifice left by one of the slaughtered demonic limbs.

Again I find myself wondering, whatever next, I thought in silent desperation. As if in answer the great heavy lids of the Guardian rolled upwards, beams of blue luminescence lancing out to fill the cavern with a mystic radiance. To the accompaniment of thunderous reports the head tilted back and its agonised visage stared up at me. Then all hell broke loose. Great tremors passed through the cavern floor, enormous fissures snaked hither and thither. Further vibrations shuddered through rock and air, the rumbling and cracking growing in intensity and volume until I was forced to clap a hand over each ear against the aural assault.

With a gut-rupturing boom the cavern floor dissolved into quivering clouds of grey splinters and the head reared upwards followed by vast shoulders, arms, trunk, waist, then legs. A few palpatatious heartbeats later the vast leviathan stood before me, its deformed visage hovering like a storm-blasted mountain crag.

I glanced far below seeking to find the portal by which I'd entered the cavern, but it had been destroyed and buried by a thousand tonnes of fallen rock. This time there was truly nowhere to go.

The great warty lips parted and a foul blast of breath washed over me, redolent with the odour of necrosis.

"You have won, *fool* wanderer," it thundered, voice like rock grinding on rock. "Come; make an end of me for I have suffered long aeons." So saying it leaned closer still, tilting its head to one side so that a vast expanse of its scabrous neck was exposed to my sword.

Questions tumbled through my mind: could it be done; was this just a trick and if I succeeded, how should I escape the cavern?

"*Come* I say, I grow impatient," the Guardian rumbled.

I glanced at its rotting face, the sores and boils, the ulcerated temples. The vast orbs of its eyes glowed with blue light, beautiful and intense, yet not strong enough to hide the sclerotic vessels webbing those ruptured surfaces. I looked again at the exposed neck, glanced at my sword, besmirched with the ichor of the demon-limbs. Pity awoke inside me for a creature whose origins were lost in the mists of time, now grown so ancient and infirm that every inch of its being was crumbing and failing. After aeons spent alone in the heart of this absurd sphere, a mortal outsider, no more than a fruit-fly in lifespan or stature, was poised to end its days.

"I cannot kill you," I said in a voice scarce more than a whisper.

"You *must!*" the Guardian insisted.

"I cannot."

"What stays your hand?" it demanded.

"Pity, compassion..." I began.

"If you felt true compassion you would slay me at once, for I have suffered more than any being alive in this world."

"No. I fight to defend myself, but you no longer threaten me. And life is sacred, even yours."

"Did not you seek me out to wreak *revenge?* I am Master of this world, thus are the mole-men my creatures. They slew your love, or is that such a little matter now? Have at me; vengeance is thine!"

Again I shook my head. "It's true, I wanted to slake my anger in such an act, but now that I stand before you I find the furnace that fired my feud-lust has grown cold."

The Guardian straightened its head and regarded me with those terrible orbs. Then it came closer and I sensed that my end was come. All fight had gone out of me and I bowed my head acquiescing to doom. The dread mouth hovered inches from me and the rough surface of those vast lips brushed against my crown, almost knocking me over.

I glanced up, astonished. Had the Mega-Giant-Guardian of Glammeth just *kissed* me?

"You need not fear me, my friend," it boomed. "Beyond all difference of scale and beneath this repellent veneer *I* am just like *you.* We are the *same*, Peachy, in our fears and wretchedness we are both prisoners to mortal angst and unwilling players in the age-old tale. Your choices here have earned you reprieve and more; you shall have the Secret of the Spheres of Glammeth. Come now; let me take you to my heart."

Though it scarcely seemed possible, the Guardian began to grow again, his body expanding in all directions while the cavern silently extended to accommodate his increasing stature like some vast placental bubble. When his colossal chest was level with me the inflation ceased and the outlines of an ordinary wooden door appeared over the place where his heart should be.

"What now?" I asked in alarm, though I think I had a fair idea.

"The secret has always lain within, Peachy. If you're honest..."

"...I've known that all along," I finished for him.

"Yes. That door is your portal to the truth. Do not delay, take it before it vanishes. You will only get one chance!"

I willed my vessel closer until it lay alongside the door and, sword sheathed, my hand closed about the brass knob. It turned with the sound of grating metal and the door, stiff on rusted hinges, opened unwillingly. Beyond was darkness.

"I don't know..." I began.

"What? Afraid? After all you have seen and endured? If you do not go on where will you go? Forward is the only path. Courage, Peachy!"

4. The Secret

The Guardian's rumbling words seemed to bear me forward and before I knew it I was passing through the open portal into velvet night. The instant I crossed the threshold all fear and discomfort left me; I sensed at once that I was falling, slowly and gently, a dandelion seed upon the musty air of summers long past.

Far below a tiny circle of light appeared, growing as I drew closer until I began to distinguish details of a dreary chamber. A grey man was sitting directly in my path, ensconced in a large grey armchair. When my descent ended, I was hovering directly above him, gazing down upon the crown of his head.

I took in the scene: skin, eyes, hair, chair, walls, every inch of the man and his surroundings was painted in the sombre palette of oxidised lead. Well, not exactly everything; in a broad circle about his chair the floor was obscured beneath brightly coloured metallic objects, each buckled and bent so as to catch stray beams of the meagre light. After contemplation I recognised them to be crumpled and discarded beer cans.

Aha! I thought, without for the life of me being able to understanding why.

Below me the man was still, his skin the mottled hue of wet ashes. I was certain he must be dead, yet no sooner had that thought flickered through my mind than he breathed a deep bronchial sigh, angled back his head and gazed up at me; a ponderous movement that seemed to require great effort of him.

The face that greeted me was deeply lined, the jaw slack and, dark as coal, his eyes were as windows on a wasteland.

I am slight, yet heavy, heavier than lead, so weighted down I can scarcely move at all. My throne is a prison from which escape is but a forlorn dream.

The words were faint, as if mumbled upon an evening breeze long ago. Was this his way of speaking? I hadn't see his lips move; perhaps I was dreaming?

His head grated forward again so that he was staring directly ahead, as he had been when I arrived.

No strength, no energy, no will. I am neither alive, nor dead. Existence is pain, yet despite wounds that will not heal I cannot die.

I had to understand this situation more completely. Descending the last few decimetres into the chamber, I took up a lotus position mere millimetres above the Grey-Man, there to consider his surroundings. The room was no less dismal from this slightly improved perspective, but now at least I could clearly see through a very large oblong window to his left. It afforded me a view of what I suspected was a sort of inner-outside-place; an esoteric skybox, put there to create the illusion of scale and depth.

Beyond thick glass, permanently fading light dominated a sombre, twilit world. As my eyes adjusted I detected the outlines of a muddy, waterlogged garden. Black trees, to which a few rust-yellow leaves still clung, crowded out the world beyond as surely as any palisade. And above the scene graphite skies trundled by.

Something was prowling among shadows and sodden leaves. I squinted and the outline of a huge dog came into view; darker than midnight its eyes were like sinkholes. I fancied that I could hear its agitated panting, smell the hot breath and slobbering chops. The hound was tormented by the Grey-Man's scent, doomed to circle the garden in hopeless chase without ever locating its quarry.

Can't go out there! the Grey-Man murmured somewhere in my mind.

"No," I agreed and then, looking around, realised the room had no door.

"Leaving in any shape or form would seem to be an impossibility, unless you can fly," I said, glancing up to assure myself the opening was still there and discovering to my horror that it was not.

Peachy Gizzard And The Spheres Of Glammeth

"Oh hell, where do I go from here?" I swore aloud. In direct answer to my question a circular hatch opened in the top of the Grey-Man's head; the nameless point again. The Grey-Man, his room and all its contents began to grow or perhaps I shrank. Whichever it was I soon found myself descending into the earthy, chill, dark of the Grey-Man's interior from which his living room prison was only visible through two ellipsoid windows.

"These windows are too small," I complained. "I can't see more than a tiny fragment of your grey chamber, and that's much too little to make any sense of."

If I had been hoping for a reply I was to be disappointed. Indeed it occurred to me that because I was now within him, my thoughts and words had in principle become his.

Were there any advantages to this odd wearing of another's shell? Perhaps. By possessing him, much like an invading spirit, I might be able to animate his body. Could I use him as a protective suit; smash my way through the window?

I tried and failed to make a single atom of him budge. His body was of such a vast weight that he might as well have been composed of ultra-dense deuterium. And far from possessing *him*, the Grey-Man's unwieldy frame in fact possessed *me*, becoming every bit as much the prison of my soul as the grey world was a dungeon to his body.

"I've been *deceived!*" I groaned aloud. "Guardian, you treacherous, dog; there's no secret here! Like a fool I walked straight into your trap, and all of my own volition."

A vibration passed through the dank, stale capsule that was the Grey-Man. I squirmed and fretted; had I just felt the thrum of distant laughter? Grinding my teeth in rage and frustration I swore that whatever it took I *would* escape.

An agonising internal manoeuvre showed me the skull hatch had closed, just like the roof shaft before it. I could not now extricate myself from the Grey-Man nor move him, nor pass out through any orifice, though I begged him to spew me back into that grey room. What then *could* I do?

Nothing.

A cocktail of despondency and despair overtook me and in moments uneasy sleep had me pinned down in inky embrace.

I dreamt of an old woman-man, begging bowl in hand, seated naked on the steps of a moss-covered Sikhara temple. Piebald skin hung slack upon its wizened frame, which possessed one withered breast, one shrivelled labia, one shrunken testicle and one half of a neatly cloven flaccid penis. A very strange sight it has to be said.

"Why are you here?" it asked me, eyes twinkling from a labyrinth of wrinkles.

"I'm lost, I think," I replied.

"No, you're not lost," the woman-man disagreed, mirth tinging its ancient voice.

"But I *am* a prisoner," I suggested.

The woman-man shook its head a smile stretching its dry and scaly lips.

"What then?" I asked in exasperation.

"Yes, *that's* the question," the woman-man agreed.

"Won't you help me?" I asked.

"Won't you help yourself," the woman-man asked in return.

"Sure, I'd love to, I just don't know how," I countered, irritation creeping into my voice.

The woman-man extended its begging bowl and arched its fleecy eyebrows.

"Oh, but I don't think I have anything...wait, what's this," I murmured rummaging through my pockets and drawing forth a string of beads. They were ugly things, brown, ivory and black like a row of bad teeth. "What on earth?"

The woman-man took the beads from me and laid them in its bowl with a rattle.

"These are things you no longer need, Peachy," it said treating me to a series of nods and further smiles. "Be silent now and listen well for I am going to tell you what you want to know.

"Deep in the belly of the unconscious mind lies the Omega point of the Self. I speak of the origin point where the four winds are born and from which all things proceed. It is the seed-heart, the centre of the labyrinth and from it issue many affects that filter up through the strata of mind. One such effect is second-hand consciousness, which is the only awareness that many human minds experience. We might dub this Consciousness as Creature.

"This Creature Consciousness is but a puppet, subject to the joint dynamics of that which takes place without and the influences of the immediately preceding layers of mind. Those layers eventually lead back to the central place, but unfortunately have a distorting effect on the pure message of the core. When creative forms of Creature Consciousness gaze back into the deeps of mind, they see the curious shapes of the unconscious and in so doing, witness the future in preparation, though generally without any insight."

Totally bewildered I wanted to interrupt the old woman-man, but found my mouth fused shut and my tongue at one with my palate as surely as if they had been welded together.

"The secret to liberation from this unsatisfactory state is the expansion of Consciousness until it becomes one with the Self. When that occurs consciousness is no longer second-hand, instead it transcend into the condition of *being* in the infinite *now*.

"*HmmmMMMhhmmMMMMMMwaaa!*" I mumbled, desperate to express my annoyance and frustration.

"Yes, yes I know, you don't understand," the woman-man nodded.

"Try this then: when the tortoise wished to see its shell it turned around, but in so doing the shell turned around with it. The view which then greeted the tortoise's curious eyes was of that which had previously been behind. However, the shell, which was still keenly sensed by the tortoise, was nowhere to be seen. How could this state of affairs come to pass, it wondered, perplexed? Frustrated it set off into the wider world in search of the shell it knew to exist, but could not find. And for many years the hapless creature looked everywhere. Yet despite knowing that the shell was close at all times, it never even caught a glimpse. And this is what is meant by the saying: *riding the ox in search of the ox.*

"A man who deemed himself cleverer than the tortoise devised a way for his body to remain facing the same direction whilst he turned around inside it. In this way he was able to stare at the place behind the one where his eyes had been.

"When he first achieved this there was to begin with only darkness. But after a while an entire world came into view and he found what he was looking for. Outside of him other people saw the strange blind man with the empty eye-sockets, who did nothing but stand perfectly still and unspeaking. They took pity on him, feeding him and helping him to drink."

The woman-man stopped speaking and fixed me with a knowing stare.

"And that's it?" I asked confounded.

The woman-man nodded, smiled and made a dismissive gesture with its wizened piebald hand. My audience was at an end.

Peachy Gizzard And The Spheres Of Glammeth

I awoke to the interior of the Grey-Man and reflected on what I'd been told, then I put the advice into practice, swivelling about inside the leaden sleeve. It was a task that proved far from easy.

When, after great effort, I was gazing in the opposite direction I found nothing but darkness, just like the man in the story. So I waited and waited, but no fantastical world materialised and before too long impatience got the better of me. I commenced the painstaking process of swivelling back, which proved even more arduous than before.

Returning to what I felt sure was my original position I discovered something was different. All I could see was a limitless field of darkness and two small elliptical points of light located very close together. They were shrinking. With a start I realised these were the Grey-Man's eyes and that they were drawing further and further away.

By turning around within I'd set in motion this withdrawal and descent and now I was picking up speed, plummeting into the heart of the innermost interior.

Deceived again, another trap; on this occasions by a damned piebald woman-man!

This time there was no mocking rumble to accompany my plunge into darkness, only weighty silence. I continued falling. The eyes receded to tiny pinpricks, remote stars on a vast sable firmament. Then they winked out, leaving me alone in cosmic night, still falling, steadily, softly, silently. Falling.

Agitated thought and anxious wondering continued for a time, then faded away. Only I remained, a speck of interstellar detritus adrift in the universal abyss. I fell and yet somehow I did not. Perhaps only I had changed and all else remained the same, I knew not. Distinctions were of no accord and concepts held no more meaning.

Years passed, decades, centuries, millennia. Even time and space were without significance. To all intents and purposes I had stopped in everything but being.

In realising this I landed and waking from the dream, gazed upon dawn with the eyes of a child. I was sitting beneath a tree, ancient and strong, its branches spreading out above me, leaves like glossy emerald teardrops. The sky's pale sapphire vault was an ocean across which shoals of spiralling clouds sailed like white horses on the spirit-sea. Sun rising: rose crescent, orange ovoid, yellow-white disc. It transformed the sky to diamond and sent out the spears of dawn, great radial fingers of illumination that encircled the world.

Peachy Gizzard And The Spheres Of Glammeth

In the grass something glinted, a piece of crystal, a perfect sphere. I picked it up and found it cool and soothing to the touch. Something stirred within its glittering core. Moving the stone closer I saw details of another world within. I brought it nearer yet and saw more until, placing it right by my eyes I became trapped within the crystal sphere and the new world swallowed my vision, making me the sole witness to its entirety.

I tried to remove the sphere, but could not. There was no hand to answer my call for action, nor other limbs nor body nor face nor even crystal ball any more. No person sat beneath an ancient tree, no sun spears crossed a diamond sky. There was only one world, entire and complete and I *was* that world.

When the winds blew I felt them blowing through me, when the land shook, it was my corpus that trembled. When the tides ebbed and flowed I became more shore and more sea. I was day and night as the sun and moon described the steps of their dancing within me. Just as I could see all the world at once, I *was* all of these things at once, and the motion of an entire world formed the foundation of my stillness.

I'd travelled through the Sphere of Glammeth, descended through the Guardian, and then through the

Grey-Man, fallen through a hole that pierced all the worlds. I had followed the stream to its source and become the worlds through which I'd fallen; now in completion I dwelt in gaps between overlapping pulses of time; the multitude within the one.

And thus I remained for all time in stillness and motion, fullness and emptiness. Whole in content, whole in process, whole in time. Seeing all, being all, my eyes the eyes of the cosmos, in ultimate being.

And yet from one state to another and in a single precipitate shift my completion unravelled. Somehow, from some unknown cause, change occurred and I was tipped out over the horizon of events. Once more I shifted from eternal gaps into pulsing temporal surf and all that was formerly whole and complete, unfolded all around me.

I still remained more one with the world than not, but found my vision narrowing to a particular focus. A detail separated itself from the whole. Within me on a tiny plane, stood the microscopic figure of a man. He stood stock still, staring ahead with sightless eye-sockets. And in him I recognised the weathered frame of one I used to know: Peacham Gizzard

Peachy Gizzard And The Spheres Of Glammeth

Had I, an entire world, once been that little man? How could I ever have been so small?

The answer came unbidden, for the detail that had separated itself from the rest of the world, now filled my eyes, and those eyes were the eyes of a man set within previously sightless sockets.

I opened my eyes and found myself in a stone-floored hall in a building that artfully combined Corbusian forms and traditionalist elements. Sunlight angled low from windows cleverly integrated into complex stone walls. I was seated on a divan and opposite me sat a young woman, her florid expression, pale-blue eyes and golden curls turned coppery in the late afternoon sun.

"Gloria?" I murmured.

The young woman started as if emerging from a dream. She yawned, stretched, glanced about her.

"But Peachy, I thought you'd left already; in fact I thought I had?" she said softly, still half asleep.

"Gloria, do you see now?" I asked, my voice soft.

She nodded. "I think so, more and more," she confirmed.

"What do you see?"

"That deep in the belly of the unconscious mind lies the Omega point of the Self. But there is nothing that is deep, nor is there a mind, there is no thing. Like the man in the story I find that there is no person in the place that is not behind the eyes, that is not a place."

I wept then for I knew what must follow, but my tears were also of joy. And at long last I knew my journey was over and that I had come to the Secret of the Spheres of Glammeth.

"Let us embrace," I said. And we rose to our feet, moving together, meeting one another, becoming one. And as our bodies merged the light of the sun flared about us in a golden cocoon. For a brief span we stood revealed as the rejuvenated woman-man, our piebald skin shining, each of us half of a perfect whole. Then feathers sprouted across our frame and we raised our arms-become-wings to take flight.

The attendant cleared his throat and glanced at his watch.

Time to close.

An intense flash of light flared up dazzling him and his ears filled with crackling and hissing.

What the blazes is happening? It seems to be coming from the next hall where that odd couple were sitting!

Peachy Gizzard And The Spheres Of Glammeth

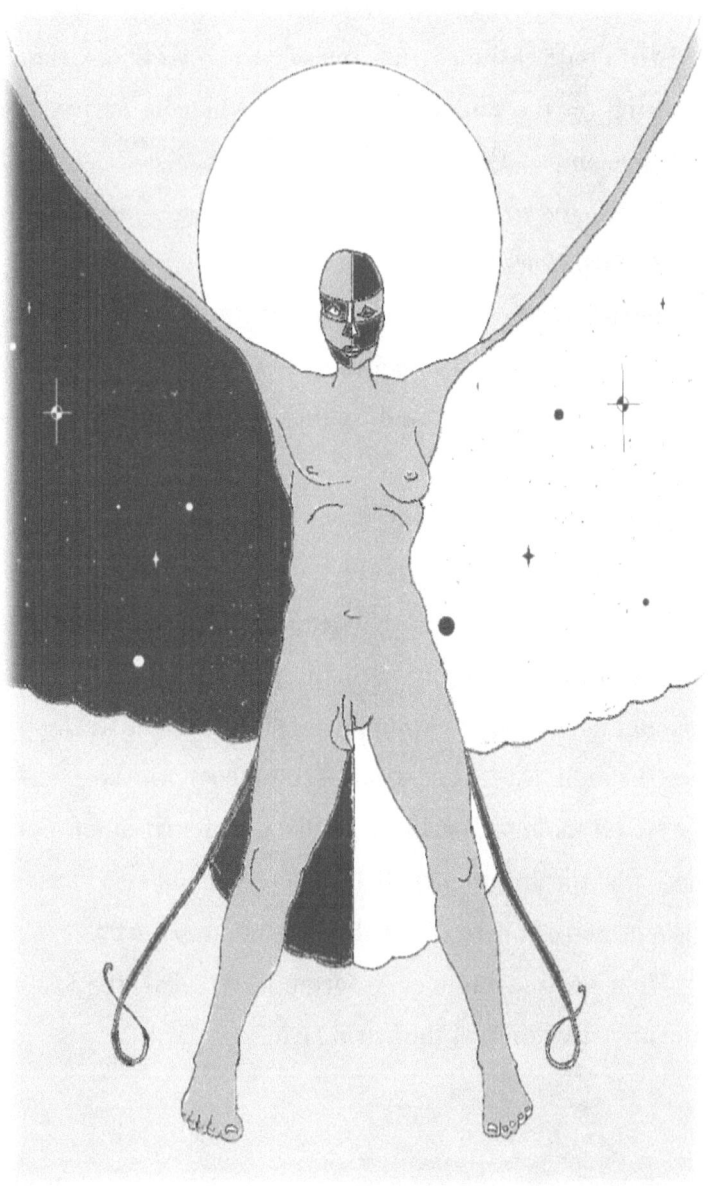

Still half blinded he moved to investigate, shoes clacking on the polished floor. But when he arrived the hall was empty. Unless...

Is that the silhouette of a bird fluttering against one of the tall windows?

Bewildered he squinted against the glare of the sinking sun, blue lights still dancing across his vision. The bird appeared both black and white; some sort of magpie perhaps?

And it was on the inside.

However do they get in here?

Shaking his head, he wandered to a concealed cupboard and opened it with his pass. Next he flicked a switch and servomotors hummed briefly. The bird flapped out through the open window into cool air beyond. It hovered a moment, perhaps revelling in its freedom. For a mere instant an eye of polished jet fixed his own through the sun-glare and an avian shadow fell across him.

Then, calling out once in farewell, the bird streaked off like an arrow toward the setting sun.

END.

ABOUT THE AUTHOR:

Andrew Coulthard Lives In Sweden With His Family. When Not Writing He Spends Much Of His Waking Time Ruminating On The Metaverse, Exploring The Mountains Or Eating And Drinking More Than He Should – Sometimes He Does These Things All At Once.

ANDREW COULTHARD

Morbidbooks Is A Grotesque Bizarro Ballet Where The Most Profane Things Occur. An Impious And Perverse Dwelling Of Dark Revulsion. A Cozy Cottage Where Torture Porn And Brutal Bible Tales Are Devised. A Quiet Place To Relax And Spin Tales Of Depravity And Wickedness. A Halfway House For The Disturbed Where Rules No Longer Apply. A Safe Haven For Deviant Serial Killers To Hatch Their Wretched Schemes. Bring Your Pets. The Tasty Ones Are Always Welcome.

HTTPS://WWW.MORBIDBOOKS.WORDPRESS.COM

ALSO AVAILABLE FROM MorbidbookS
IN PRINT & KINDLE:

HE HAD TO HAVE HER THE MOMENT HE SAW
her trachea ring. Six months later she was his lovely wife.
He performed his duties as a husband and she as a wife.
He tolerated a house filled with references to her late first
husband and the children they had together. He put up
with her prudish ways. He waited. He was patient. He
planned. He was adaptable. He was rewarded over the
course of a week in her basement. He turned his perverse

sexual fantasies of worms and maggots and her lovely crusty trachea ring into a gruesome reality.

A DIRTY SHAMEFUL DEVIL OF A SECRET...

Something that two men share. A legacy that will shock you to your very core. One that is created not out of madness, but of the purest desire. Take a vivid journey into the mind of the killer and his biggest fan. Do you believe in evil? See the knife plunge. Lap at the wounds. Do you still? There is no rational meaning or pretty words that will hide away the darkness that the words of this found journal creates. Inside is the real truth. And it can

set you free. Watch all you want. Taste what you dare not
have. But once you see, you are in collusion. Keep reading
and the guilt will stain. No longer can you feign
innocence. The change is as permanent as it is wretched.

"The Routine has this inherent tendency to perpetuate
lies, and I speak only in thinly veiled euphemisms —
hanging out with friends means going to the bar; being
tired means too many sleepless nights on amphetamine;
going grocery shopping means robbing Price Chopper
blind; filling a prescription means visiting my dealer;
going to the bank means pawning my possessions — but

refer to them not as "lies;" rather, label them as weak excuses utilized to justify my erratic behaviors.

Not that the distinction between lies and excuses even matters. My locations and actions mean little to the lives that I infect, for I manipulate my stories into such bizarre versions of actuality that no one seems to question their authenticity, thereby validating my words under the general principle that facts are stranger than fiction. Besides, the language of lies often involves a certain element of truth, mere embellishments of the life that I dream to live – all-night hotel parties, never-ending supplies of coke and meth, hundreds of dollars to spend frivolously, high-class bars at expensive ski resorts, private chemists and personal chauffeurs, fame and fortune, and immunity to the consequences of my behaviors."

HUMANITY IS THE DEVIL IS A DECONSTRUCTED nightmare mixing David Lynch and snuff movies. The plot revolves around a central character, Seth, who is set about a crusade against humanity which, for him, represents pure evil. Through random killings he and his cronies try to accelerate the end of the world, in order to provoke and defeat the Demiurge, the false God that is ruling the earth. As in Burroughs, logical language is replaced here with cut-scenes – sometimes to be taken literally – that plunge the reader into an extreme experience. Both incredibly morbid and enthralling, HITD is a masterpiece of moral darkness and existentialist reflection upon our comfortable religion and morals.

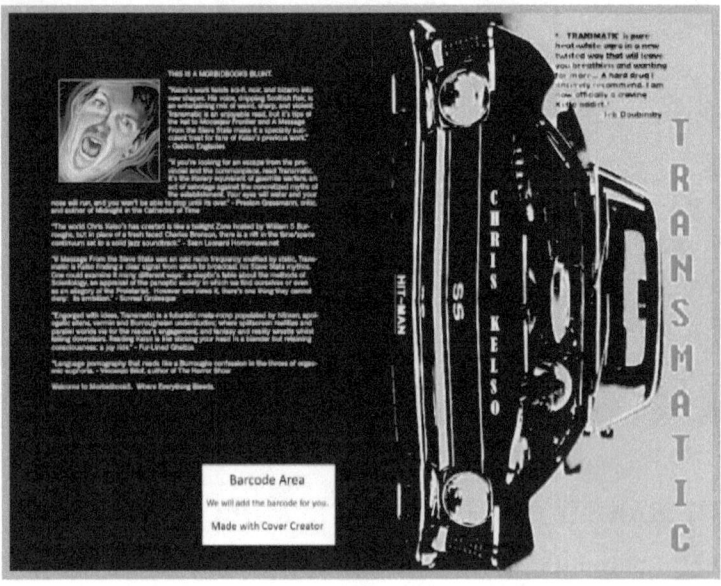

"AS A PART-TIME HITMAN/ EXTERMINATOR,

Ignius Ellis's dream is to buy a candy-apple red Nova Supreme. In the process of trying to earn enough cash to make his dream come true he gets sucked into the rough world of Visitacion Valley, SF. When the tenants in his apartment complex reveal their various extracurricular activities this take an even more bizarre twist and Ellis soon becomes acquainted with the nightmarish Slave State dimension..."

THAT'S THE LAST TIME SHE GETS THE BIGGER WORM... Once their flesh flakes away the angels collapse into puddles of hissing goop and withered petals blow into them hurried along by unseen winds. My spit looses its sweet taste to the black flavor of ash. The glowing birds in the bright orange sky burst into small sparkly novas. The sky itself weeps and tears, streaking down like a ruined painting as the dismal gray of life wheezes back before my eyes. I don't blink; praying silently for one last desperate sensation of the high. Lila feels it too. She writhes on the mattress next to me; her moans of ecstasy warping into groans that capture the hollowness of our souls. Tears form in her eyes and I can almost feel the lump in her throat. It's gone and she wants to cry. I'd rather chase down more Worms than cry about it but everybody reacts to the Worms differently. I slip away to my own neon colored utopia where things with wings fan me and comfort me when the living neon worm dissolves under my skin. Lila told me once they wrap around her like a giant fuzzy neon hug. I imagine her high shedding off her like snake skin and flaking to the filthy floor next to the mattress. Her high sounds better than mine. More Fun. That's the last time she gets the bigger worm.

Peachy Gizzard And The Spheres Of Glammeth

"IF YOU KNOW WHAT KINBAKU, POST-IMPRESSIONISM, and brilliant green eyes have in common, then you are probably a fan of Alex S. Johnson! Congrats! But if you don't know, allow me to open the door, guide you inside, and introduce you to a little Wicked Candy. This is a sweet designed for the discerning Bizarro fan's tastes, and I promise, you will not be disappointed!"
--Mimi Williams, author of Beautiful Monster

"A short collection that both traverses the genre lines and melds them together into one masterpiece. Jam packed with horror, laughs, pop culture history and more, this one is a must have for lovers of the macabre, the bizarre and the hilarious."
--Jeff O'Brien, author of Bigboobenstein

IN GARRETT COOK'S MURDERLAND serial killers are idolized by society. Their deeds are followed obsessively by television pundits and the adoring public. A subculture has grown up around this phenomena, called "Reap." Laws are created to allow this activity to flourish, including designated "safe zones' where killers can practice their trade without fear of persecution. Fans of the top rated serial killers celebrate each new kill on social media and television. Programs glorify their deeds. The culture of Murderland is violent and mirrors our own violent society and its decadent obsessions; but Murderland isn't about how violent the world has become.

Peachy Gizzard And The Spheres Of Glammeth

It's about the pervasive nature of media and how it
corrupts. It corrupts absolutely.

At the heart of Murderland is Jeremy Jenkins. Jeremy
doesn't like what he sees and he's just enough insane to
believe he can do something about it, that he can change
the world. His methods are extreme- to outdo the serial
killers, he'll kill THEM, turn their own twisted reality
back on themselves. It's a hopeless task, impossible,
Herculean; but it's Jeremy's fate to see it through to the
end.

The three sections of Murderland comprise a true
Homeric epic. In the first section we are shown the
terrible world Jeremy lives in, the world that if we look at
it honestly, is really our own world. We meet all the
principal characters, the serial killers, the pundits, the
pawns, and Jeremy's beloved Cass. In the second section
Jeremy goes on a bit of a spiritual quest and comes to
understand his true purpose. In the final section the
flames are ignited and all hell breaks loose. Jeremy, like a
great epic hero must journey to the underworld and be
reborn in order to triumph.

BORN WHOLE FROM THE RECTUM of a dying
patient, Morbid silently stalks the hospital's hallways,
heinously dispatching the most helpless of patients and in
the most painfully repulsive of manners. In the meantime,
in order to pay for his family and home that includes his
ghost step-father Sammy and his pet aborted fetus Chip,
Westphal has to ingest mounds of dangerous narcotics to
get through his night shifts. Barely hanging on to his
Care Tech gig by his fingernails, the last thing Westphal
needs is to be accused of Morbid's evil deeds. You, on the
other hand, simply want to find some solace. Terminally
ill from a virulent infection, and dependent on Life

<u>Peachy Gizzard And The Spheres Of Glammeth</u>

Support, all You beg for a peaceful and dignified demise.
Shirk has other plans for You. The ancient drug-
snuffling demon makes You relive all of your deadly and
venial sins as he tortures You. Night after night. Until
eternal Damnation begins for YOU MORBID
WESTPHAL, yet again....

IT LOOKS LIKE CAROLYN AND MARK

are in deep, deep shit...

Mark and Carolyn live in an alternate 1989 where Ronald
Reagan is on his fourth presidential term. The USA has a
rigid, long-standing caste system and abortions were never

made legal. Being homeless is a crime that is punishable by imprisonment in an internment camp the inmates call Tent City. Most of Mark's ER patients are inmates at this camp and are victims of a new disease these illegals call the Transient Flu. This deadly and rapidly spreading disease mutates with each new host, collecting information, changing code. The disease evolves lightning quick, spreading like pond ripples and infecting everyone. No one is safe. Mark and Carolyn dig too deep and uncover the brutal truth: Transient Flu was purposely made and is one hundred percent fatal. Carolyn's employer, Hudson-Smythe Pharmaceuticals, discovers the chain of evidence. It traces the pharmacide back to Hudson-Smythe and the crime of the century. Cost is no object and deadly force is authorized. Yes. Carolyn and Mark are in deep, deep shit.

Peachy Gizzard And The Spheres Of Glammeth

IMMANUEL THE CHRIST HAS SOME NERVE.

Jonah has already lost everyone he loves to Pilate the
vampire and his Harbor drug violence. Jonah now trudges
through his days staying as high on Plata as possible. He
just wants to be left alone while he waits for his turn to
die. The Christ has other plans for him. She sends Her
messenger, Pedro, to assign Jonah the very dangerous task
of ordering the Herod to dismantle the Harbor's Plata
trade. Jonah decides to run. But you can't run from God
forever. As Jonah learns the hard way when the 'Edmund
Fitzgerald' founders and goes down in rough seas, with
the reluctant prophet on board.

ANDREW COULTHARD

www.ingramcontent.com/pod-product-compliance
Lightning Source LLC
Chambersburg PA
CBHW020628130626
46552CB00003B/1122